ANIMALS in the OUTHOUSE

Written by Anja Fröhlich
Illustrated by Gergely Kiss

SKY PONY PRESS

Sky Pony Press • New York

At first glance, you might think this day is like any other day in the forest. The sun is shining. The trees are blowing in the breeze. The flowers are bright and beautiful. But wait a minute! What is that big ugly blue thing sticking out of the grass on the top of the hill?

Why, it's an outhouse! It's the kind they have at the main lodge so that tourists can go to the bathroom. But tourists don't come to this part of the forest very often. Only the animals use this lovely meadow at the edge of the forest. Why would anyone put an outhouse out here?

The answer to that question is simple. The new forest ranger wanted to impress his boss. As he was looking around for a project, his dog Hector showed up with rabbit poop on his paws. Then a tourist complained about some strange smells in the forest. That did it! The brilliant idea came to the ranger in a flash. Why not install an outhouse for the animals so they wouldn't be making such a mess of the forest?

The wild boar, Professor Grunter, was the first to find the outhouse.

"Aha, ahoink, it seems we have ourselves an outhouse," he muttered. He prided himself on his problem-solving ability and soon figured out that the lid lifted up and that you're supposed to sit on the round part beneath it.

"Verrry interesting," he mumbled to himself. "I'll be the first to use this thing so the other animals will be able see how clever I am."

But the more he thought about it, the more the outhouse worried him. Did he really want to be the first to try to sit on that hole? What if he fell into those deep dark depths below? Nope, he was not going to take the chance. He'd just tell everyone he used it, and then see what would happen when another animal came along.

Professor Grunter spread the word of his success in the outhouse. In no time the admiring animals assembled in front of the plastic hut, chanting, "Way to go, Professor Grunter!"

Not wanting to be outdone by Professor Grunter, Billy the
bear pushed forward to be the next one to use the outhouse.
After all, as the biggest guy in the forest, he was not afraid of
anything—least of all a little blue outhouse!

And so he worked very hard to impress the others. He stuffed his huge body into the little hut and squashed his great fat bottom onto the little seat. But Billy was so large that the blue plastic outhouse almost burst apart! The other animals had to use all their strength just to keep the door shut so that Billy wouldn't come rolling out.

Billy was not happy. In this position he couldn't do what he was supposed to do. But he didn't want all the other animals to know that he was not able to use a perfectly normal outhouse.

He opened the door and, looking the picture of success, called out,
"Next, please!"

"Way to go, Billy!" shouted his friends.

Prickly the hedgehog was next in line. He had a very different problem. For him the little outhouse was not too small. It was far too big! He wasn't even able to see the toilet seat, much less figure out how to use it. It must be up there somewhere, but how was he to reach it? Hedgehogs can't climb walls! But he didn't want to admit to the world that he was not capable of doing something as simple as using an outhouse. On the other hand, he did not want to lie to his friends. He'd never been in an outhouse before, so he saw no harm in informing them, "That's a fabulous outhouse—the best one I've ever been in!"

"Way to go, Prickly!" shouted his friends.

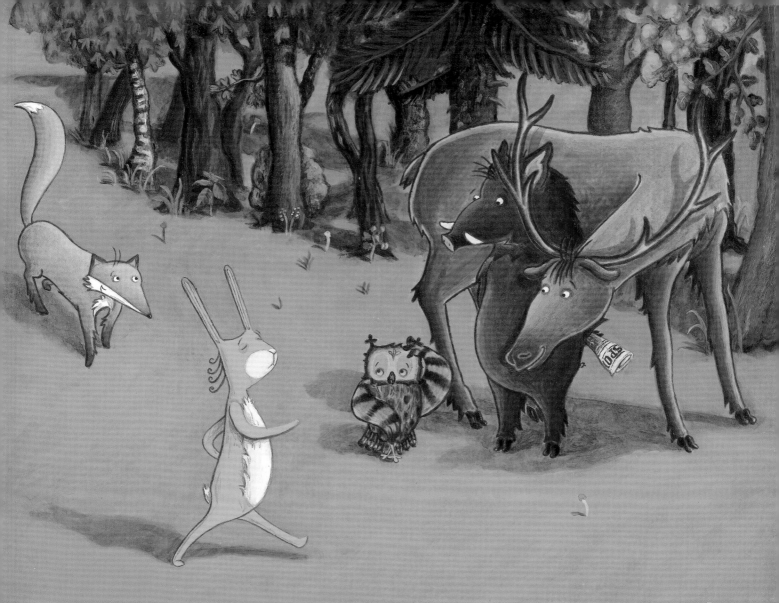

For Harriet the hare, the outhouse was just the right size. With an elegant leap, she jumped onto the seat and waited for all the little pellets to fall down into the depths below. But nothing happened. Then Harriet remembered that her stumpy tail always had to be tickled by a few blades of grass before she could poop. Without a grassy tickle, she simply couldn't use the outhouse for what it was intended.

But she did not want to tell the world about needing to be tickled. Harriet considered that information very personal. So she stepped out of the outhouse, with a somewhat snooty look on her face, and said, "It is about time we animals had a decent lavatory. After all, here in the forest we're all very civilized, are we not?"

"Way to go, Harriet!" shouted her friends.

"If Prickly and Harriet can do it, then it'll be no problem for me," thought Fancy the fox to himself, and strutted confidently into the little hut. A few moments later, he marched out again with the same that-was-no-problem look.

But anyone with an eagle eye would have seen at once that Fancy also had
his troubles. When he sat down, his wonderful bushy tail dropped down into
the depths and got soaked with water—or whatever else. Yuck! That upset him
so much that he just wanted to get out of the outhouse. "The inventor of this
thing obviously didn't think about those of us with beautiful, long, fluffy tails.
How dumb," the fox thought to himself. But of course he was not going to say
that to anyone else. He did not want to draw attention to his wet tail and, more
importantly, he didn't want to be the only failure in the forest.

Next in line was Stanley the stag, who could just about get his body into the little hut, but unfortunately not his antlers. He had no choice but to leave his antlers sticking outside the door.

Now anyone who has sat on the potty with his head out of the door would know exactly how embarrassed poor Stanley felt.

"All of you turn around and cover your eyes with your paws and claws," he cried. But Stanley still didn't feel comfortable. Rather than admit defeat, he cried, "Finished!"

"Way to go, Stanley!" shouted his friends.

The next outhouse guest was Olive the owl. She could not understand what to do with the seat, which is understandable. Owls don't exactly poop like other animals. They get rid of a lot of their waste by coughing up pellets and spitting them out.

"This thing just isn't designed right," thought Olive to herself. "There's no way I'm sticking my head in there. I'm just not doing it!"

Professor Grunter was the last in line. Fortunately everyone else had left by now. In fact, most of them left rather in a hurry—heading for their favorite pooping spots in the forest, no doubt.

"They all thought the outhouse was wonderful, so I guess I should use it myself," thought Professor Grunter.

But he didn't feel very happy at the thought that so many others had already been in the outhouse before him. That would mean an enormous mix-up of smells. If another wild boar were to come along, he wouldn't even be able to tell that this was a safe place for a boar to poop.

Then the clever professor had an idea. He removed the seat and the lid and carried them to his favorite place. He laid the seat on the grass in a clearing that smelled of wild boar and nothing and no one else. Now he could sit there comfortably and read his newspaper and not worry about a thing.

At first sight anyone can see that today is unlike any other day.

As the sun rises, all the animals crowd together excitedly at the edge of the forest. The ranger is driving the blue outhouse away.

At the spot where the outhouse was standing yesterday, there's now a sign. It shows a little blue outhouse with a red X over it.

"So is everyone free now to do what she wants to do, and do it wherever she wants to do it?" asked Harriet the hare. "Are we going back to where we were before? Back to those bad old outhouse-less days?"

She sounded quite annoyed, and all the other animals pretended to be annoyed as well.

Of course the ranger couldn't hear these protests because his tractor was making far too much noise. But that didn't matter because he knew perfectly well that the animals did not like the outhouse at all. When he came to see how things were going, he did not find anything at all in the outhouse—in fact, he couldn't even find the seat!

The ranger realized that each of the animals had his or her own way of going to the bathroom, and none of them needed a human outhouse. And anyway, Hector's new galoshes solved most of his problems. In fact, a new idea was forming—what about issuing shoes or boots to all the forest animals…? Mmmm….

Way to go, Ranger!

Originally published as *Müssen Wir? Eine kleine Klogeschichte* by Verlag Friedrich Oetinger, Hamburg, 2010.

Sky Pony Press books may be purchased in bulk at special discounts for sales promotion, corporate gifts, fund-raising, or educational purposes. Special editions can also be created to specifications. For details, contact the Special Sales Department, Sky Pony Press, 307 West 36th Street, 11th Floor, New York, NY 10018 or info@skyhorsepublishing.com.

Sky Pony® is a registered trademark of Skyhorse Publishing, Inc.®, a Delaware corporation.

Visit our website at www.skyponypress.com.

Manufactured in China, January 2012
This product conforms to CPSIA 2008

10 9 8 7 6 5 4 3 2

Library of Congress Cataloging-in-Publication Data is available on file.

ISBN: 978-1-61608-659-6